NEW HAVEN PUBLIC LIBRARY
W9-AJP-997

E OHI
Chicken, pig, cow on
 the move /
35000094785184
MAIN

Chicken, Pig, Cow
On the Move

Ruth Ohi

annick press
toronto + new york + vancouver

©2009 Ruth Ohi (text and illustrations)
Design: Sheryl Shapiro and Ruth Ohi

Annick Press Ltd.
All rights reserved. No part of this work covered by the copyrights hereon may be reproduced or used in any form or by any means - graphic, electronic, or mechanical - without the prior written permission of the publisher.

We acknowledge the support of the Canada Council for the Arts, the Ontario Arts Council, and the Government of Canada through the Book Publishing Industry Development Program (BPIDP) for our publishing activities.

ONTARIO ARTS COUNCIL
CONSEIL DES ARTS DE L'ONTARIO

Cataloging in Publication

Ohi, Ruth
          Chicken, pig, cow on the move / by Ruth Ohi.

"A Ruth Ohi picture book".
ISBN 978-1-55451-194-5 (bound).—ISBN 978-1-55451-193-8 (pbk.)

          1. Chickens—Juvenile fiction.   2. Swine—Juvenile fiction.
3. Cows—Juvenile fiction.   I. Title.

PS8579.H47 C45 2009   jC813'.6   C2009-900840-8

The art in this book was rendered in watercolor.
The text was typeset in Billy.

Distributed in Canada by: Published in the U.S.A. by:
Firefly Books Ltd.   Annick Press (U.S.) Ltd.
66 Leek Crescent   Distributed in the U.S.A. by:
Richmond Hill, ON   Firefly Books (U.S.) Inc.
L4B 1H1   P.O. Box 1338
                                   Ellicott Station
                                   Buffalo, NY 14205

Printed in China.

Visit Annick at: www.annickpress.com
Visit Ruth Ohi at: www.ruthohi.com

For Annie, Sara, and Kaarel.

—R.O.

Chicken, Pig, and Cow loved their barn.
They loved best friend Dog.

But sometimes things
seemed a little crowded.

"Excuse me," said Cow to Chicken,
"but you're standing on my hoof."
"Well," said Chicken, "you're squishing
my tail."
"Well," said Pig, "you're wearing mine."
Chicken gave Pig his tail back.

"We need a change," said Pig.
"We need more space," said Chicken.
Cow didn't say anything.

Pig found the first home.

But it was too linty.

Cow found the second home.
But it was too scary.

Chicken found the third home.
"It's perfect," said Chicken.

"I've always wanted my own bed," said Cow.

"I've always wanted my own slide," said Pig.

"I've always wondered what TV was like," said Chicken.

Night came.

"Goodnight!" yelled Cow.

"Goodnight!" yelled Pig.

"I'm trying to sleep!" yelled Chicken.

Cow curled up.
She lay on her side.
She lay on her back.

She lay wide awake.
"Goodnight, Dog," whispered Cow.

Pig peeked out his window.
Many faces peeked back.
"Hello," said Pig.
But no one answered.
"Do you know Dog?" asked Pig.

Chicken lay on his couch.
He stared at TV.
TV stared back.
"Woof," said Chicken.

Chicken found Cow.

And Pig.

"Good thing we have all this space," said Cow.

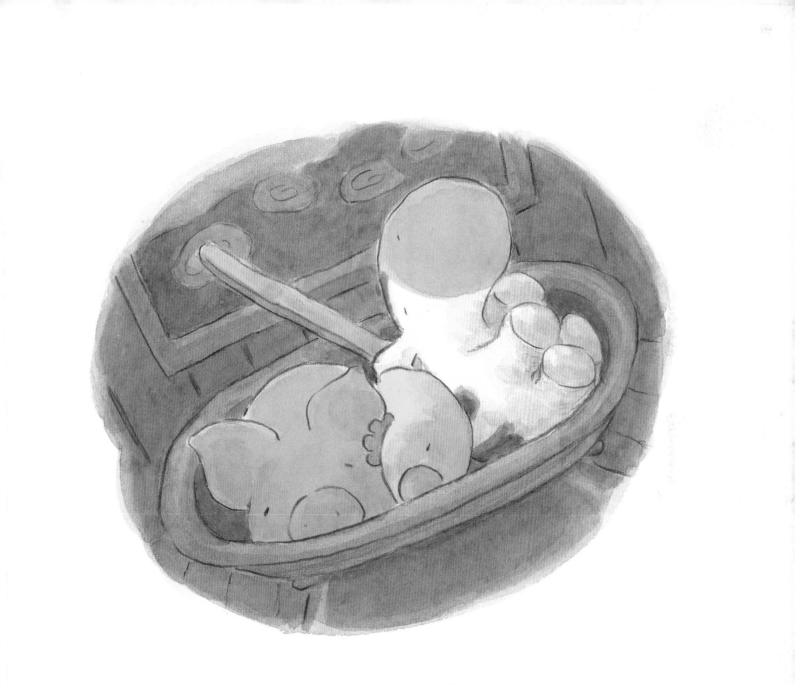

Chicken, Pig, and Cow fell asleep.

Morning came.

So did Girl.

"Houses don't fly," said Chicken.

"I think sometimes they do," said Cow.

"How do we get home now?" said Pig.

Chicken pointed.

"Fetch!" said Chicken.

When Dog came back, he had the barn.
"Good Dog," said Chicken.
"Thank you, Dog," said Cow.

Chicken, Pig, and Cow loved their barn.
They loved best friend Dog.
And when things got crowded inside, they loved
getting out—for a little adventure.